An Easter Egg Hunt for JESUS

God Gave Us EASTER to Celebrate HIS LIFE

by Susan Jones

Illustrated by Lee Holland

Good Books

New York, New York

A quiet *forest* wakes up from its winter sleep. Buds blossom and trees stretch their branches. It's a special day today!

The *friendly*
Owl *flies* over
the treetops.
"Happy Easter!"
he hoots to the
forest below.

"It's time for the Easter egg hunt, Little Bunny," Mama whispers.

"Make sure to keep an eye out *for* the most special Easter egg," says Badger.

All the animals begin to search high in the tree tops and low in the meadows.

Eggs big and little, bright and pastel, are tucked into their hiding spots.

Little Bunny hops and hops until he *finds himself* in the flowering meadow.

He scurries through tall grass, wrinkling his nose as he searches for the most special Easter egg of them all.

Little Bunny's heart takes a leap when he spots a clearing in the meadow. Could it be?

"I don't think I'll ever find an egg,"
Little Bunny says glumly.

With the sun shining and the chatter of his friends off in the distance, Little Bunny continues on.

They're probably *finding* Easter eggs!

Little Bunny hops. And hops.
And hops. And–*crunch*.

Just beneath his *feet*, Little Bunny sees the brightest, most special Easter egg he has ever seen . . . *broken!*

"Did you find the special Easter egg?" Little Hedgehog and Little Raccoon squeal, springing out from behind the tall flowers.

"No, I *ruined* the special Easter egg," Little Bunny says with tears in his eyes.

"Oh, no," they sigh sadly. With
fallen faces and worried hearts, the
three friends leave the meadow.

"I'm sorry, Mama, I broke the special egg," Little Bunny says sadly as he returns home.

"No, Little Bunny, you've discovered what's so amazing about it!"

"The hollow egg is a symbol of Easter. This special egg is empty, like Jesus's tomb, to remind us that He is risen." Badger smiles.

"Little Bunny, you opened the egg and showed us the miracle of Jesus's sacrifice!" chimes in Little Raccoon.

Little Bunny's whole being fills with warmth and wonder. With his friends by his side, he wriggles with the joy and hope of Jesus and the celebration of His gift to us all.

Together, these special
forest friends cheer,
"Happy Easter, Jesus!"

Good Books books may be purchased in bulk at special discounts for sales promotion, corporate gifts, fund-raising, or educational purposes. Special editions can also be created to specifications. For details, contact the Special Sales Department, Good Books, 307 West 36th Street, 11th Floor, New York, NY 10018 or info@skyhorsepublishing.com.

Good Books is an imprint of Skyhorse Publishing, Inc.®, a Delaware corporation.

Visit our website at www.goodbooks.com.

10 9 8 7 6 5 4 3

Library of Congress Cataloging-in-Publication Data is available on file.

Cover illustration by Lee Holland

Print ISBN: 978-1-68099-437-7
Ebook ISBN: 978-1-68099-438-4

Printed in China